Disney
FROZEN
FEVER

by Rico Green

Illustrated by the Disney Storybook Art Team

PaRragon

Bath • New York • Cologne • Melbourne • Delhi
Hong Kong • Shenzhen • Singapore • Amsterdam

Elsa felt excited and worried in equal measure. Tomorrow was her sister Anna's birthday – and it was the first one in many years that the sisters would spend together!

Elsa rose early, and while Anna was still sleeping, she began the preparations for the big day. She decorated the castle courtyard and used her magical powers to create a beautiful icy topper for the cake.

Kristoff, Olaf and Sven soon arrived to help. They had made a birthday banner, and they hung it across the courtyard.

Elsa tried not to panic as she watched the wet paint drip from the banner on to the tables below!

"Are you sure I can leave you in charge here?" Elsa asked Kristoff.

"Absolutely," he replied.

Elsa headed off to finish the decorations, but then she caught sight of Olaf sneaking a taste of the birthday cake!

"Olaf, what are you doing?" she asked.

"I'm not eating cake," said Olaf.

Elsa leaned close to him. "It's for Anna," she said with a smile.

Just then, the morning bells chimed and Elsa hurried inside the castle
to wake the birthday girl.

"Keep an eye on that cake!" she called to Kristoff, and dashed into
the castle.

Elsa sneaked quietly into Anna's room. "Pssst. Anna," she said.
Anna yawned. "Yeah?" she said, her eyes still closed.
"It's your birthday," said Elsa.
At first, Anna was too sleepy to realize what Elsa was saying, but then ...

... she sat straight up!

"It's my birthday!"

While Anna changed into her new birthday dress, Elsa suddenly sneezed and two tiny snowmen appeared. They were snowgies! The creatures fell to the floor and scampered away before the sisters even noticed them.

With a magical wave, Elsa added flowers to her own dress and ice sparkles to Anna's. Although Elsa's head felt a bit funny, nothing was going to stop her from making Anna's birthday really special.

Next, it was time for Anna to find her presents!
"Just follow the string," said Elsa, handing the end of it to her sister.
Anna sprinted down the hall, eager to see where the string would lead her.

Anna followed the string down the hallway ...

... and under some furniture.

She quickened her pace ...

... until she ended up at a suit of armour, where she found a beautiful bracelet! Next, the string led to a cuckoo clock. But instead of a cuckoo, it had a tiny Olaf figure which shouted "SUMMER!" every time the clock opened its doors.

"Summer!"

Next there was a huge, delicious sandwich and then
a brand-new family portrait.

The sisters were having lots of fun, even though
Elsa's sneezes were becoming more and more frequent.

Anna was worried, but Elsa insisted
that she was feeling fine.

Neither of them noticed
the tiny snowgies that continued
to appear with each
sneeze....

Back in the courtyard, Kristoff and Sven were busy with the decorations when suddenly a group of the little snowgies appeared! They stared at the tiny snowmen in disbelief.

The snowgies jumped all over the place, and made the punch bowl topple over! Elsa was not going to like this!

Olaf, on the other hand, was very excited to meet these new tiny friends!

"Ah-choo!" Elsa sneezed again as she and Anna zipped down the stairs on Anna's new bicycle.

By now, Anna was worried that Elsa had a cold.

"I'm fine," Elsa said.

Elsa had even more gifts for Anna outside the castle. They stopped at Oaken's kiosk, where its owner was busy having a sauna!

Oaken gave Anna his softest cloak, then offered Elsa a cold remedy that he said was "of his own invention".

"No thanks," Elsa said, taking a deep breath of the steamy air.

"We'll take it," said Anna.

Anna's final present was at the top of the tall clock tower.

"Now we climb," said Elsa.

"You need to rest," said Anna. But Elsa insisted.

Elsa grew more tired with every step. At the top, way up high, Elsa suddenly twirled feverishly – and almost fell!

Anna caught her poor sick sister. "You've got a fever. You're burning up," she said, determined to get her sister to rest.

Meanwhile, more and more snowgies were arriving in the courtyard and causing chaos! One group knocked down the birthday banner and Olaf had to re-hang it.

"All fixed," Olaf announced, putting up the last piece.

A second group of snowgies headed for the birthday cake. Kristoff came up with an interesting way to stop them....

But the snowgies seemed determined to destroy the cake. This time they launched themselves at it!

Kristoff had promised Elsa he would keep the courtyard in order, and he didn't want to let her down.

As the sisters reached the doors to the courtyard, Elsa turned to Anna.
"I'm sorry, Anna," she said sadly. "I just wanted to give you one perfect birthday."
"Everything *has* been absolutely perfect!" Anna said, pushing open the doors....

"Surprise!" called Kristoff.

He had managed to sort everything out just in time! Even he was amazed.

Anna's eyes lit up at the sight of the decorations, her friends and the hundreds of tiny snowgies! "Wow!" she said.

Everyone sang 'Happy Birthday', then Kristoff slid down off
Sven's antlers and knelt before Anna with her birthday cake.
Anna had a huge smile on her face.

Sven cut the beautiful cake into slices for everybody to enjoy.
Elsa was proud of all the hard work she had put into the day.
    But she felt another sneeze coming on.
    Elsa really needed to get to bed ...

... but not before doing one last thing. In Arendelle, there was a huge birthday horn, which the king or queen would blow on special birthdays. Anna tried to stop her, but Elsa was determined!

As Elsa blew into the horn, she accidentally sneezed and sent a giant snowball flying far across the ocean ...

... and right into Hans! It knocked him off his feet!

At long last, Elsa let Anna
take her up to her bedroom.
It was finally time to rest.

In Elsa's bedroom, Anna gave her big sister some warm soup.
"Best birthday present ever," said Anna.
"Which one?" said Elsa.
"You letting me take care of you," said Anna.

The sisters smiled widely at each other. It really was Anna's best birthday ever, and it was all thanks to Elsa and their wonderful friends.

High on the North Mountain, not long after the birthday party had ended, Marshmallow opened the doors of the ice palace for Kristoff and Sven. Olaf came running in, surrounded by the little snowgies! Everyone had decided the ice palace was the best place for them to live.

Kristoff looked at Marshmallow, shook his head, and said, "Don't ask."